THE RUSTY, TRUSTY TRACTOR

For Shaun and Patrick Gittard
—J.C.

For Carl—both of them
—O. D.

Text copyright © 1999 by Joy Cowley
Illustrations copyright © 1999 by Olivier Dunrea
All rights reserved

Boyds Mills Press, Inc.
A Highlights Company
815 Church Street
Honesdale, Pennsylvania 18431
Printed in China

Publisher Cataloging-in-Publication Data
Cowley, Joy
Rusty, trusty tractor / by Joy Cowley; illustrated by Olivier
Dunrea.—1st ed.
[32]p. : col. ill.; cm.
Summary: A grandfather is convinced that his rusty, trusty,
fifty-year-old tractor will make it through another haying season.
ISBN 1-56397-565-3 hc • 1-56397-873-3 pbk
1. Farm life—Fiction—Juvenile literature. 2. Grandfathers—Fiction—
Juvenile literature. [1. Farm life—Fiction. 2. Grandfathers—Fiction.]
I. Dunrea, Olivier, ill. II. Title.
[E]—dc21   1998   AC   CIP
Library of Congress Catalog Card Number 97-77970

The text of this book is set in 16-point Galliard
The illustrations are done in gouache.

10 9 8 7 6 hc
10 9 8 7 6 5 pbk

THE RUSTY, TRUSTY TRACTOR

written by Joy Cowley

illustrated by Olivier Dunrea

Boyds Mills Press

When Mr. Hill saw Granpappy's tractor, he laughed fit to bust his britches. "Woo-oo!" he cried, slapping his knees. "You call that a tractor?"

Micah looked up at Granpappy to see what he was thinking, but Granpappy was not letting on.

Mr. Hill ding-donged with his knuckles on the rusty engine cover and the spaghetti can that hung over the exhaust pipe. He kicked the old, cracked tires. "This won't last another season," he said. "Do yourself a favor, sir. Come on down to Hill's Tractor Sales and look at some new machines."

Micah leaned against Granpappy's leg, but Granpappy just scratched his neck and said, "I don't know, Mr. Hill. Me and this trusty tractor been together fifty years, ever since my old plow horse died. We know each other real good. I'm not hankering to go looking at shiny new tractors."

"No harm in looking," said Mr. Hill.

Micah tugged a handful of Granpappy's overalls. "Please? Please?"

Granpappy looked down and smiled. "Well, now, maybe just a peek wouldn't hurt that much."

"You won't regret it, sir," said Mr. Hill, shaking Granpappy's hand up and down like a pump handle.

Hill's Tractor Sales covered half a block. Micah had never seen so many tractors all in one place. There were big ones, small ones, red ones, yellow ones, some with plows, some with buckets, some with forks, and some with diggers.

Mr. Hill showed Granpappy a big red tractor with a cab like a truck. "Got carpet in there," said Mr. Hill. "Got heating and air conditioning."

"Mine's got air conditioning, too," said Granpappy. "When the air gets too fresh I put on another jacket."

"Look," said Mr. Hill. "Stereo music."

"I whistle," Granpappy said.

Mr. Hill showed them the big fancy-dancy engine, but Granpappy was not interested. He said, "When my old tractor won't go, I fix it myself with a bit of wire. None of this electronic fiddle-faddle."

Mr. Hill was not real pleased that Granpappy did not want one of his shiny new tractors. But Mr. Hill was not a man to give up easy.

"How much grass you reckon on sowing this spring for hay?" he asked.

"Twenty acres," Granpappy said.

"Well, sir, I know that you are not a betting man. But I'll give a jelly doughnut for every acre if your tractor gets through the season. If it doesn't—"

"It will," said Granpappy.

"If it doesn't," said Mr. Hill, "you come back to Hill's Tractor Sales. That's all I ask."

Come early spring, when they were setting up for plowing, Micah said, "You know, Granpappy, this old tractor is sure hard to start."

"Like me," said Granpappy. "I'm hard to start when it's cold and damp."

"Sure is rusty," Micah said.

"I know how that feels. My knees got so much rust, some days they need an oil can." Then Granpappy looked at Micah. "Boy, you aren't trying to sweet-talk me into buying a new tractor?"

Micah quickly shook his head.

"Good. 'Cause this is my old friend, and friends don't let each other down. You remember that."

The ground was still cold when Granpappy plowed those twenty acres. The tractor crawled along, *chugga, chugga, chugga,* like an old fishing boat, brown waves curling up behind the plow.

Sea gulls followed, looking for bugs and worms.

Plowing took most of three days, but when Granpappy finished, the field was a strong brown sea with waves as straight as ruler lines.

Granpappy stuffed a sack with straw because the seat cushion was worn out. "We got a long way to go yet," he said.

The lumpy earth was smoothed out, and the steel blades of the harrows cut up the soil nice and fine, ready for sowing.

Then Micah helped Granpappy with the seed drill. Grass seed went in the small hopper. Fertilizer went in the big one.

Chugga, chugga, chugga.

Micah hung on the fence and watched as the rusty old tractor pulled the seed drill round and round. Grass seed and grass food dropped into little furrows.

"Now it's up to Mother Earth," Granpappy said.

The sun shone, warm spring rains fell, and green leaves sprouted on the poplar trees.

"Granpappy! Granpappy! Come and see!"

Sure enough, the field was showing rows of new grass as fine and soft as a baby's hair.

The rest of spring came through at a gallop. There were tadpoles in the creek and birds' nests in the barn. The grass in the field grew tall and thick.

Roses bloomed, strawberries ripened. Granpappy dug his first crop of new potatoes.

Now the grass was as high as the bib of Micah's overalls.

Mr. Hill paid a visit. "Good crop of hay," he said. "But I tell you plain and simple, no way is that tractor going to tow a hay baler. It just don't have the horsepower. Now is the time to think about a new model. What do you say?"

Granpappy gave a slow, soft smile. "I say I'm mighty partial to jelly doughnuts."

The first run of fine weather, Granpappy sharpened the blades of the old mower. Micah helped him bolt the mower onto the tractor.

Chugga, chugga, chugga.

As the tractor went by, the tall grass fell and lay flat on the ground.

"In a couple of days," said Granpappy, "we'll turn it with the hay rake to help it dry."

The morning Granpappy got out the baler, the weather forecast changed. "Thunderstorms tomorrow," Granpappy said. "Wet hay is good-for-nothing hay. We've got to get ourselves cracking."

"What if the tractor breaks down?"

Granpappy shrugged. "We lose twenty acres of hay and twenty jelly doughnuts. Worse things have happened. But I tell you now, boy, real friends are there when you need them, and my old tractor won't break down."

Mr. Hill was partways right. The tractor was not big enough for the baler. But Granpappy, he talked to it like it was his favorite horse. He called it "old partner" and whistled songs to it, and that rusty, trusty tractor shuddered across that field, dragging the big baling machine.

Sweet-smelling grass got scooped up, rolled and tied, and spat out again in hay bales weighing five hundred pounds. The rolls fell down with a thump that shook the earth under Micah's feet.

The storm broke that evening. Rain came out of the sky like water from a fire hose, but every bit of hay was wrapped in bales, snug and dry. Micah and Granpappy were in the kitchen cooking up some corn chowder when the screen door rattled. They found Mr. Hill on the porch, as wet as a new-caught catfish and carrying a box of jelly doughnuts.

"I hereby declare you the winner," Mr. Hill said to Granpappy. "Though I don't know how you did it with that antique bucket of rust. Wang-a-dang, sir! You got more good luck than a hound dog in a butcher's shop."

Mr. Hill said good night and went off into the rain. But before Granpappy and Micah had gotten to taste the first doughnuts, that tractor man was back on the porch, wetter now than a heap of catfish, his feet dirty up to his knees. He wiped the water out of his face. "Excuse me. Seems like I got a problem. My car. It's stuck in the mud."

Micah looked at Granpappy and waited. Granpappy was real polite. "No problem, Mr. Hill. Me and my grandson and my old tractor will get you out in no time at all."

And would you believe it? As cold and damp as it was, that rusty, trusty old tractor started up first try.